ERIN, RODERICK, &

THE

DIFFABILITY

BUNCH

Fliss Goldsmith

Ian R. Ward

Erin, Roderick, & the Diffability Bunch
Book #2 of Erin & Roderick Book Series

Published by Purple Diamond Press 2021

Copyright © 2021 by Fliss Goldsmith

Written by Fliss Goldsmith, UK

Illustrated by Ian R. Ward

Edited by Sarah Khan

Paperback: ISBN: 978-17355372-8-3

Library of Congress Control Number: 2021913186

Purple Diamond Press LLC

Villa Park, Ca, USA

Visit www.FlissGoldsmith.com or

www.PurpleDiamondPress.com for more information

Sports day was underway, and a sad looking Erin sat with Dora. Erin was sad because she could not compete. She had broken her leg falling off her skateboard.

Dora as usual watched on, drawing everything she saw.

Mr. Patwari was rushing around as always. "I've lost the starters whistle for the sprint. We mustn't give up though!" he smiled.

Erin's brother Roderick and best friend Benji were getting ready to start the obstacle race. Benji signed to Erin.

"I'm going to win for you". Erin smiled and so did Dora.

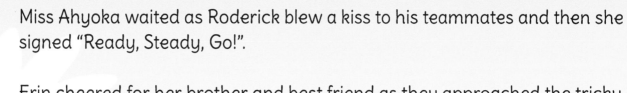

Miss Ahyoka waited as Roderick blew a kiss to his teammates and then she signed "Ready, Steady, Go!".

Erin cheered for her brother and best friend as they approached the tricky course. Dora kept on drawing silently. Dora having Autism and Mutism meant she never spoke.

5

Roderick stopped to wave to his friends but Benji stayed focussed and leaped ahead. Benji crossed the line in first place!

"Winner," he signed to Erin – she signed "Well done!" back to him.

Next up was the basketball hoop challenge and Elise was hoping for a win. She had been practising hard at home.

She was in the final two having scored eight hoops in a minute.

7

Dora drew her friend Elise, capturing her throwing the ball beautifully. Erin smiled. "You're so talented Dora," she said.

Mr. Patwari ran past again, "Still can't find that whistle and Ryan is getting rather upset. We mustn't give up though!" he spluttered.

The crowd were fixed on the action. "Good luck," shouted Roderick. He sat with Erin, Dora and Benji under the tree out of the sun.

"I wish I could join in," Erin sighed. Roderick patted her back, he knew how great his sister was at sports and how upset she felt.

Elise came over to her friends after the challenge had finished.

"Beaten by one hoop!" she shouted, "The other player is as tall as a giraffe, I don't think he even had to jump to get the ball in!".

"You were great," Erin told her, and Benji signed "Awesome".

"I totally wanted to take a selfie but there are no phones allowed," grumbled Elise.

"I really need that whistle for Ryan!" barked Mr. Patwari as he scrambled past, swiftly adding, "But we mustn't give up!".

"What's wrong with him?" asked Roderick. "Oh, he's always in a merry muddle," joked Elise, "Ryan won't run the sprint without the starting whistle."

Erin pointed to Dora's art book, "Look Elise, there's your selfie!" Elise gasped, "Oh my goodness, that is AMAZING! Can I keep it?" she begged. Dora nodded and ripped out the page for her.

Miss Ahyoka signed to Benji to ask him if he had seen the whistle. He signed back "No".

She went on to explain that Ryan was getting quite distressed as he was used to the whistle signaling the start of his race. Down Syndrome made some situations harder for him to process.

13

Erin got up onto her crutches and went to talk to Ryan at the start line. "Hey mate, what's wrong?" Ryan was going red in the face.

"It's not fair. I can win this. They've lost the whistle. This is my race."

Erin showed him how to do some deep breathing. Ryan began to feel calmer.

"Don't worry we WILL fix this," Erin reassured Ryan as she walked him over to the tree to wait with their friends.

Elise said, "Hey Ryan, what's going on?" Ryan took a deep breath, and more calmly said, "I can't run without the whistle."

Benji was staring at Dora's drawings. She had drawn Erin and Ryan chatting and an excellent one of Rod entertaining the crowd with his famous dance moves.

Ryan looked over at Dora's sketchpad and said, "You are mega clever." Dora blushed and looked down to the floor.

Mr Patwari stopped at the group and sadly told them, "I can't find the whistle, I'm so sorry." He dashed off to speak with Miss Ahyoka and the group of friends sat silent.

"This is silly!" Elise blurted out, "We can fix this, we always find a way to fix our problems." Benji gave a thumbs up and the rest of them nodded in agreement.

Dora scribbled something on a bit of paper, ripped it out and slipped it into Erin's hands. As Erin read the note she began to smile.

"We've got a plan. Ryan get to that starting line!"

"Yes!" Ryan punched the air with delight and raced to his position. Dora and Erin smiled at each other.

Dora packed her art things into her bag and steadily walked Erin over to Mr Patwari and Miss Ahyoka who were at the starting line.

Smiles rippled across the teachers' faces.

Erin turned to Dora and said, "Your plan is brilliant – it'll help Ryan AND me. Thanks for keeping me smiling today, you're a great friend." Dora smiled and looked at the floor. The sprinters lined up.

Ryan was ready to go. "I've got this!" he shouted to the crowd and they cheered for him. Ryan was always lightning quick, and it was going to be hard for the others to catch him.

Dora stood and helped Erin lay down her crutches. She put her arm around Erin's waist to steady her on her broken leg. As the crowd fell silent, Erin turned to the runners and shouted,

"You will go on MY whistle." Then she lifted her fingers to her mouth and let out the loudest whistle you have ever heard!

Immediately Ryan had taken a clear lead. Another runner was close but, as they neared the line, Ryan knew in his heart that he was going to win this.

"**I did it !**" he screamed as he flew over the line, "YES!"

He struck a hero pose and listened to the cheers.

Dora helped Erin back on to her crutches and all the friends grouped together at the finish line.

They were so proud of Ryan who was working on making Down Syndrome his super-power. He was certainly a hero to them.

Mr Patwari and Miss Ahyoka came to thank the courageous kids and told them there was cake and juice back at the Fanzone tent for everyone.

Elise clung with pride to her picture as Dora pushed her towards the tent. Benji signed "I'm starving" to Ryan who beamed and shouted happily, "Me too, let's go!"

Erin and Roderick stood and watched their fabulous friends.
"Today was a great day," Roderick told Erin. "Yes, much better than I
thought it would be," she replied.

"You know, we all have different abilities don't we – and that's
awesome," Erin noted. Roderick agreed. As they headed to the tent, he
exclaimed,

"We're the Diffability Bunch!" and Erin thought her brother was
absolutely right about that.

Let's Talk About It...

Deafness

In our story Benji is Deaf. This means that he cannot hear anything. As such, people are using Sign Language to communicate with him. Sit for a minute and thing about what it must be like to go through a day without being able to hear. Do you know any sign language? It's awesome that there are so many other languages! Could you try and learn Sign Language? (Go to www.cbeebies.co.uk and search Makaton)

Autism

Dora is described as having Autism but what does that mean? Autism affects the way someone understands the world around them. It may mean they struggle to communicate and behave in ways that are different. They may struggle with lots of noise or people. They can be incredibly talented at things like Art, Maths and Music. What talents do you have?

Mutism

Dora is also Mute, which means she does not speak. Dora's Mutism is part of her Autism. As you can see though, she is an amazing artist and draws what is happening around her. How would you communicate if you did not speak? Dora uses her abilities to overcome her challenges. Can you think of times you have overcome a challenge?

ADHD

Roderick's character struggles with concentration and has ADHD. It can make children shout out, talk over people and be unable to sit and focus on an activity. Not everyone with concentration difficulties has ADHD. As you can see Roderick's energy is brilliant and he loves his friends. What do you love about your friends?

Wheelchair Use

Elise uses a wheelchair as she was born without the use of her legs. Have a think about all the things you use your legs for. Elise has strong arms from whizzing around in her awesome wheelchair. She has learned to do all the things her friends can do. How can you offer your help to a wheelchair user? What do you think Elise's other talents are?

Down Syndrome

Ryan has Down Syndrome. For people with Down Syndrome, it sometimes takes longer to learn things. They also grow at a slower rate than children without Down Syndrome so are often smaller than their friends. Ryan sometimes struggles to communicate his feelings. Down Syndrome does not stop children from being part of friendship groups or being great at things. What do you notice that Ryan is great at?

Erin – Erin's challenge is not a permanent one. Her broken leg will heal. What do you think she struggles with? What do you think she will have learned from this sport's day?

Thanks for being a part of the Diffability Bunch – You are all welcome here.

'This book is dedicated to 'Mamty', because she knows and shows that love really is the answer – always '

xxx

***May you be so kind and
write an Amazon Review.... and check out***

Erin & Roderick Discover Families
This book is set on a super sunny afternoon where they are taking a picnic and playtime in the park with their friends and of course their family. As the children and the adults soak in the sunshine Erin and Roderick begin to wonder what exactly 'Family' is -

With my Love

L. Goldsmith x.

Lightning Source UK Ltd.
Milton Keynes UK
UKHW050254260721
387725UK00002B/10